A Gift For:

_____

From:

_____

Copyright © 2013 Hallmark Licensing, LLC

Published by Hallmark Gift Books,
a division of Hallmark Cards, Inc.,
Kansas City, MO 64141
Visit us on the Web at Hallmark.com.

Editorial Director: Delia Berrigan
Editor: Nate Barbarick
Art Director: Jan Mastin
Designer & Production Artist: Bryan Ring

ISBN: 978-1-59530-964-8
LPR1661

Printed and bound in China
JUL13

Snow Time to Lose
The Shiverdale Snow Buddies Save the Day

By Diana Manning
Illustrated by Mike Esberg

In the village of Shiverdale, Finny O'Flurry

is somebody everyone knows—

he's a likable snow-guy whose little dog Rex

is with him wherever he goes.

Now, Rex has a habit of getting in trouble.

He really does WANT to be good,

though sometimes the way that he tries to help out

just doesn't turn out like it should.

Finny is patient, and brings him along
when he goes to rehearsal each week,
where he sings with his pals in the Shiverdale chorus—
their music is really unique!

The chorus is known for their Christmas Eve Sing-Along,
held every year on the square—
snow-kids and snow-families join in the singing,
and everyone wants to be there!

"It's a Christmas tradition for folks far and near,"
their director says, proud as can be.
"It's a very big deal, so let's be at our best—
we've got to make sure we're on key!"

When practice begins, Finny sings from the heart . . .
while his little dog Rex really HOWLS.
Stopping the music, the stern Mr. Trebleclef
grumpily grumbles and scowls.

"That dog has to go!" he finally declares,
and throws his baton in the street.
But Rex thinks they're playing a fun game of fetch,
and carries it back in his teeth.

Patting his head, Finny sends him on home,
with the promise of treats later on—
Mr. Trebleclef sighs as he turns to his chorus
and takes up his icy baton.

"We've got to be ready! Our honored guest soloists
both will be joining us soon!
Snowphie Soprano and Baron von Yodel,
arriving by hot air balloon!"

Their journey turns out to be freezy and breezy—

poor Snowphie holds on to her hat.

Von Yodel looks over their flight plan again

so he can make sure where they're at.

They land on the roof of Trebleclef's house,

where they'll stay as his holiday guests.

"We're honored to have you!" They're greeted with smiles.

"Won't you come in and just rest?"

The very next day when it's time for the Sing-Along,

Trebleclef's nowhere around.

Finny and Rex go to knock on his door

and find icicles down to the ground!

Poor Mr. Trebleclef's trapped in his house
along with the soloists, too—
"Our hot air balloon must have melted the snow!
Now what are we going to do?"

"We've got to get out," Mr. Trebleclef shouts.
"We can't disappoint all our fans!"
Soon everyone hears of their icy dilemma
and comes to help out with a plan.

They try to break through, but the ice is too thick,
and they wonder what they should do next—
when Finny O'Flurry declares, "Not to worry!"
and calls for his little dog Rex.

Popping his head from a snowbank nearby,

the lovable Rex reappears—

"Not HIM again," Trebleclef loudly protests.

"That dog has been trouble for YEARS!"

Then Finny starts singing, with Rex joining in
with an ear-splitting howl of a sound—
it rattles the ground, and they hear a big CRACK!
as the icicles all tumble down!

"There's no time to lose!" Mr. Trebleclef shouts.

"The Sing-Along's ready to start!"

So he and the soloists rush to the square,

while already singing their parts.

The Shiverdale Sing-Along happens as planned,
and everyone's really relieved—
the crowd gives a cheer and surrounds Rex and Finny
as heroes who saved Christmas Eve!